To my Superhero Dad, with love

T. K.

For Mega-Matilda, Bionic-Bea, and

Magic-Martha, from Dynamo-Dad x x x

J. B.

Text copyright © 2015 by Timothy Knapman
Illustrations copyright © 2015 by Joe Berger

Nosy Crow and its logos are trademarks of Nosy Crow Ltd. Used under license.

First U.S. edition 2016

Library of Congress Catalog Card Number 2015937228
ISBN 978-0-7636-8657-4

15 16 17 18 19 20 GBL 10 9 8 7 6 5 4 3 2 1

Printed in Shenzhen, Guangdong, China

This book was typeset in Gaspar.
The illustrations were created digitally.

Nosy Crow
an imprint of
Candlewick Press
99 Dover Street
Somerville, Massachusetts 02144

www.nosycrow.com
www.candlewick.com

SUPERHERO DAD

TIMOTHY KNAPMAN

illustrated by JOE BERGER

Dads are
sometimes boring,

but **mine's** not,
and I'm **glad,**

because,
you see,

he's secretly a . . .

HAM!

I can hear his **Super Snoring**

from a thousand miles away . . .

so I jump up on his bed and shout,

"Come on, let's start the day!"

ZZZZZZZZ

Then he makes a
Super Breakfast,
though he's only
half awake.

The very best is
toast with **chocolate,**
and fruit, ice cream,
and **cake!**

His jokes are
Super Funny . . .

and his laugh is **Super Long.**

HA HA HA Ha Ha Ha Ha Ha Ha HA HA!

He can pick up our dog, Jumbo, so he must be **Super Strong.**

Whenever we play dinosaurs, he does a . . .

oOOoOOOAR!

like this.
And afterward he gives
me a tyrannosaurus kiss.

When he **zooms**
me up and down,
I feel like
I can **fly.**

And when I'm on
his shoulders
I am **taller**
than the **sky.**

He's super good
at woodwork, too
(he MEANT to
bang his thumb).

He **saws**
and **hammers**,
glues
and **paints**,
and makes the
wood become . . .

"But HOW is he a **Superhero?"**

people sometimes ask.

"He wears his briefs **inside** his clothes and **doesn't** have a **mask!"**

Well, some nights,

when it's dark and late,

I think I hear a **noise**

that sounds a lot like

monsters

hiding somewhere

near my **toys.**

I call out "Dad!" but quietly,
so the monsters cannot hear . . .

"**Superhero Dad,**" I say,
"you are the **best** by miles!"

My dad says,
"I'm no **Superhero**,"
then he stops and smiles.
"But I know a **Superhero**
who is brave and kind and fun.

Who is it?

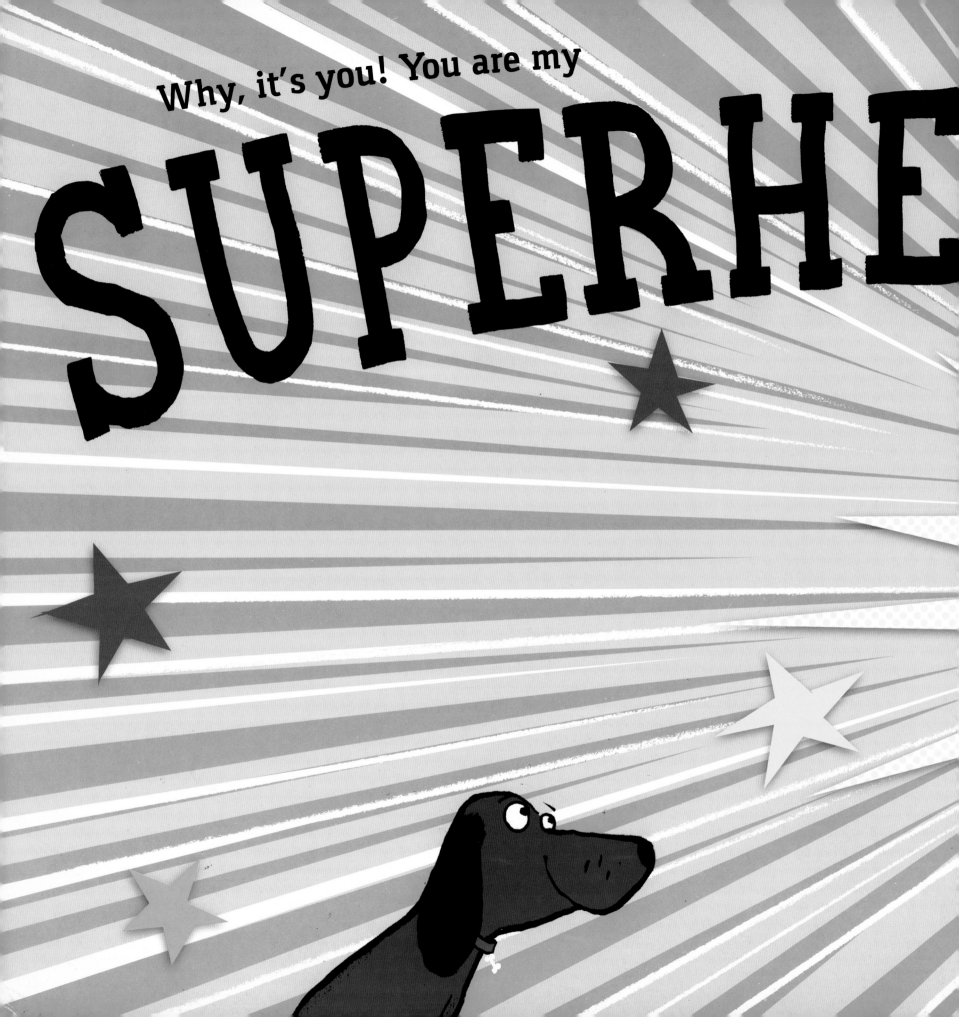

Why, it's you! You are my

SUPERHE